Happy Burpday, Maggie McDougal!

by Valiska Gregory

Illustrated by Pat Porter

SPRINGBOARD
B·O·O·K·S
®

Little, Brown and Company
Boston Toronto London

With thanks for support from the Indiana Arts Commission, the National Endowment for the Arts, and the Butler University Department of English and Writers' Studio

Text copyright © 1992 by Valiska Gregory
Illustrations copyright © 1992 by Pat Porter

First Edition

The characters and events in this book are fictitious. Any similarity to real persons, living or dead, is coincidental and not intended by the author.

Library of Congress Cataloging-in-Publication Data

Gregory, Valiska.
  Happy burpday, Maggie McDougal! / by Valiska Gregory ; illustrated by Pat Porter—1st ed.
    p. cm.—(Springboard book)
  Summary: Having no money and seeing her best friend's birth-day approaching, Maggie creates a package of homemade and recycled items, hoping Bonkers will not be disappointed when he realizes his present is second-hand.
  ISBN 0-316-32777-8
  [1. Birthdays—Fiction. 2. Gifts—Fiction. 3. Friendship—Fiction.] I. Porter, Patricia Grant, ill. II. Title.
  PZ7.G8624Hap   1992
  [Fic]—dc20   91-27507

10 9 8 7 6 5 4 3 2 1

WOR

Published simultaneously in Canada
by Little, Brown & Company (Canada) Limited

PRINTED IN THE UNITED STATES OF AMERICA

For Grams and her grandchildren:
Melissa and Holly
Robert and Kenneth
Eric and Becky

1

Big Trouble

" 'Strike three, and you're out!' " shouted Maggie McDougal. "That's what the umpire said."

"Then everybody started jumping up and down like crazy," said Bonkers. He stuffed another oatmeal cookie into his mouth.

"It sounds like fun," said Grams, smiling. Maggie liked the way her grandmother's eyes crinkled at the edges like her cookies.

"Oh, it *was* fun," Maggie said. "Those tickets to the White Sox game were the best

birthday present you ever gave me, Bonkers. Thanks."

Bonkers bowed and tipped his baseball hat. "You're welcome."

"Bradford, isn't *your* birthday coming up soon?" Grams asked.

"Yep," said Bonkers. "It's on Saturday, and I'm having a big party. I hope somebody will get me a Green Lizardman Space Station, but my mom said I shouldn't count on it."

After Bonkers went home, Maggie didn't say anything for a long time. Finally, she sighed loud enough for Grams to hear. "Oh, Grams," she said, "I am in BIG trouble. I have to buy Bonkers a birthday present, and I spent all my money on hot dogs at Comiskey Park."

"What if you thought of a present that doesn't cost money?"

"I can't buy a Green Lizardman Space Station without money," said Maggie, "and I have to have a really good present after what happened last year."

"If I remember right, you insisted on getting Bonkers a Princess of the Planets flashlight because that's what you wanted for *your* birthday."

Maggie nodded. "And he got me a Green Lizardman cape because that's what he wanted for *his* birthday."

"But you worked it out."

"Sure," said Maggie. "We just traded presents. But this year it's not going to be so easy."

Grams gave Maggie a hug. "If I know you," she said, "you'll think of something."

Maggie McDougal hoped that Grams was right.

2
That Cynthia

On Tuesday, Maggie McDougal stood in the recess line with Bonkers. They were holding their lips still as they talked. Their teacher, Ms. Chumley, didn't like it when they talked in line, so they talked through their teeth like wooden puppets.

"I can't wait until Saturday," said Bonkers.

"I know," said Maggie. Her mouth was so still it looked as if it were painted on.

"Class," said Ms. Chumley, "I hope that's not talking I hear."

Cynthia squeezed in between Bonkers and Maggie. "The birthday present I'm bringing you is so big I can hardly carry it," she whispered.

"Then I'm glad I invited you this year," said Bonkers.

Maggie thought about Cynthia. She had curly hair and always had the biggest of everything. "You don't have to brag, Cynthia," said Maggie like a puppet.

"You shouldn't talk in line," Cynthia said through her teeth.

Maggie was so mad she forgot to hold her lips still. "I am not talking in line," she said out loud.

Ms. Chumley frowned. "Maggie McDougal, go to the end of the line, please. You know you are not supposed to talk now."

Cynthia stuck out her tongue as Maggie walked to the end of the line, but Ms. Chumley didn't see her do it. It wasn't the first time Cynthia had gotten Maggie in trouble.

That afternoon, Ms. Chumley told the class that they were going to begin a unit on families. Maggie wasn't sure what a unit was, but she knew Ms. Chumley liked units a lot.

The class was just finishing a unit on flowers. They had read stories about flowers, they had counted flower petals, and now they were working on their flower poems. Bonkers gave his poem to Maggie to read.

Flowers
by Bradford Hamilton Williams III

Some flowers are pink and
some flowers are blue.
When they fall apart,
you need some glue.

Bonkers seemed happy when Maggie laughed at the glue part. Ms. Chumley said Bonkers's poem was interesting and put a sticker of a petunia at the top.

Maggie was proud of her poem. She had looked long and hard at a dandelion and tried to write exactly what it was like:

The Dandelion
by Margaret Ellen McDougal

The dandelion stands tall
and wears a yellow button hat.
Then later, it's all fuzzy-headed,
and it blows wishes in the wind.

When Ms. Chumley stepped out of the room, Cynthia grabbed Maggie's poem off her desk. She read the poem loud enough for the whole class to hear. Then she whispered something to Jenny, and they laughed.

"I did not write a funny poem," Maggie said. She felt her cheeks getting hot.

"I didn't say it was funny," said Cynthia. "I said it was stupid. Whoever heard of a flower wearing a hat?"

"It's not exactly wearing a regular hat," said Maggie. "It just sort of looks like a hat."

"And dandelions don't blow wishes," Cynthia said. "*People* make wishes, not dandelions."

Just then Ms. Chumley walked back in the class and everybody got quiet.

"That Cynthia," Maggie whispered to Bonkers. "I don't like her one bit." Maggie felt all wilted, like a dandelion without its fuzz. Bonkers tapped her arm and slipped her a note. It said:

Maggie,
 I liked your poem a lot.
   Your friend,
   Bonkers

Maggie smiled. Maybe, she thought, Bonkers would like a poem for his birthday. Then she thought about the present Cynthia was going to bring and decided she'd better think some more.

3
Blicky

That night, Maggie McDougal showed her poem to her mother and father. She told them what Cynthia and Bonkers had said.

"I think it's a fine poem," her father said.

"And it was nice of Bradford to send you that note," her mother said.

"And that's exactly why," said Maggie, "I need extra money to get Bonkers a really special present." She put a piece of bread on her brother Mikey's high-chair tray. He cheerfully gnawed on the crust like a puppy.

Maggie smiled hopefully at her parents. "What Bonkers really wants is a Green Lizardman Space Station."

"Didn't we just give you some extra money for Bonkers's present?" her father asked.

Maggie squirmed in her chair. "Yes," she said, "but I sort of spent it at the baseball game." Her father and mother looked at each other.

"Maggie McDougal," said her mother, "you were *not* supposed to spend that money on yourself."

"I know," said Maggie. "What I don't know is what I'm going to do about it." She put some peas and a blob of mashed potatoes on Mikey's tray.

"Blicky," said Mikey.

"Not blicky, Mikey. Potatoes are good," said Maggie, even though she didn't feel like eating anything herself. "If I say I'm sorry," she asked her parents, "couldn't you just give me more money?"

"Definitely not," said her mother.

"Maybe Grams could give me some money?"

"Definitely not," said her father.

Mikey put a spoonful of mashed potatoes on his head. "Tick," he said, waving at Maggie.

"That's a good trick, Mikey," she said and gave him a quick smile. "I may as well warn you," she said to her parents. "If I don't get Bonkers a really good present, he may kill me. You may never see your daughter again."

"I'm sure you'll think of something," said her father.

Maggie wished her parents were a little more worried about never seeing their daughter again. "I could wash dishes and mow the lawn," she said. "I could scrub the floors just like Cinderella."

"I'm sorry, Mags," said her mother, "but we have already given you your allowance for helping around the house, and we've warned you before about budgeting your money."

"Maggie McDougal," said her father, "it's not the first time you've spent all your money before you thought. This time, we're not going to bail you out."

Maggie was beginning to feel like a mashed potato herself.

"You don't have to have a lot of money for a good present," her mother suggested. "When we were first married, your father spent only fifty cents and gave me a whole garden of marigolds for my birthday. It was a wonderful present."

"That would be great if Bonkers liked marigolds or if I had fifty cents," said Maggie.

"Maybe you could write Bradford a poem. He liked your dandelion poem a lot," suggested her father.

"I thought about that. But I think Bonkers would like a poem for his birthday present about as much as he would like lace underwear."

14

"You'll have to do the best you can, Mags," said her mother.

Mikey stuck out his tongue. It was covered with peas and mashed potatoes. "Blicky," he said.

"You can say that again," said Maggie, and Mikey did.

4

Family Trees

On Wednesday, Maggie McDougal stared at the board. *If only* I didn't have to go to school, she thought, I could get a job to make money for Bonkers's present.

Ms. Chumley passed out manila paper to each row monitor. "Today, class," she said, "we are going to draw our family trees."

"My family doesn't have any trees," said Jenny. "We live in an apartment."

"Just follow directions," said Ms. Chumley. "When you get your piece of paper, I

16

want you to draw a large tree like the one on the board."

Maggie looked at Ms. Chumley's tree. It looked like a cloud sitting on top of a Popsicle stick. Ms. Chumley talked about how families grew like trees, and then she drew a line on the board. It looked to Maggie like a diving board in the middle of the tree cloud.

"I have one sister," said Ms. Chumley, "so I am going to draw two lines on this branch of my family tree." She drew two little lines so the diving board looked like a table with short legs. They all drew diving boards with short legs in the middle of their tree clouds.

"Now," said Ms. Chumley, "I am going to put my name and my sister's name on our family tree." She wrote SALLY underneath one table leg and GRACE underneath the other.

"Now you try it," said Ms. Chumley. She walked around the room as they wrote.

If only I had a big sister on my family tree, thought Maggie, she would probably loan me money for Bonkers's present.

Ms. Chumley stopped at Bonkers's desk. "But Bradford," she said, "you don't have a sister named Sally."

"I don't have a sister named Grace either," Bonkers said.

Ms. Chumley sighed. "Class," she asked, "how many of you put SALLY and GRACE on your papers?"

Nineteen hands waved in the air. Then Ms. Chumley explained that they were not supposed to put SALLY and GRACE on their papers. They were supposed to write the names of their *own* brothers and sisters under the table legs.

"My sister's name is Patricia Teresa Maria Schwartz," said Jenny. "Can I just put PAT?"

"Just put PAT," said Ms. Chumley.

"My mother is pregnant," said Frank, "and I don't know the name of the new baby yet."

"Just put a question mark," said Ms. Chumley.

met an *if only* that could solve a problem."

Maggie thought about all of her *if only*s. "Maybe Grandpa was right," she said finally. "My *if only*s haven't done a thing for me so far."

"Why don't you give yourself a break from worrying and keep Mikey company while I set the table?"

Maggie handed Mikey his red truck.

"Tuck," said Mikey. "Grrr."

"Good boy, Mikey. Truck." Maggie had long ago given up trying to explain to Mikey that trucks didn't growl.

Bonkers did like my poem, Maggie thought. I suppose the least I can do is make him a card. "Bonkers's card needs to be funny," she said, as if Mikey could understand. "And what would really be nice is a card that's gross. Bonkers loves gross stuff."

"Mmmm!" said Mikey. He started chewing on the wheel of his truck.

Maggie giggled. "People don't eat trucks,

Mikey." She gave Mikey a drink of juice from his tipsy cup, and he rolled over on his back like a bear cub. He started making what Maggie called his blubby noises, and then all of a sudden, he burped.

It was a loud burp, and Mikey smiled as if he had just won a prize.

"Good boy, Mikey. That's a happy burp!" Maggie stopped short. "Grams—I've got it!" she said. She gave Mikey a quick hug and put him in his high chair.

Maggie drew a giant sandwich on a piece of folded paper. Then she rummaged through Grams's Good Stuff Box. Grams loved recycling things, and the box was filled with old keys, screws, used tinfoil, sequins, string—all the things Grams couldn't bring herself to throw away.

"Think succotash," Maggie said to Grams. "A little bit of this and a little bit of that, and this will be the best card Bonkers ever got."

"Can you use this leftover glitter from the

signs I made for the recycling center?" asked Grams.

"Definitely," said Maggie. She found some brown buttons in the bottom of the Good Stuff Box. "Pepperoni," she announced, "and I could use this yarn for spaghetti."

When she had finished gluing everything on the card, Maggie opened the refrigerator and took out a jar of pickles. "Think of this as a homemade scratch-and-sniff card," she said. She carefully dipped each corner of the card in pickle juice.

Mikey banged on his high-chair tray.

"Look, Mikey. Bonkers is going to love it!"

Mikey wrinkled up his nose. He looked at the green-glitter pickle shining in the middle of the giant spaghetti-pepperoni-pickle sandwich. "Mmmm," he said.

"Now for the best part," said Maggie. On the inside of the card she wrote in big letters, HAPPY BURPDAY!

6

Heirlooms

On Thursday, Maggie McDougal saw a large box on Ms. Chumley's desk, and on the board in big letters was the word HEIR-LOOMS. "Does anyone know what an heirloom is?" Ms. Chumley asked.

Only Cynthia raised her hand. "An heirloom is something handed down in your family."

"Very good, Cynthia," said Ms. Chumley. "Let me give you an example, class." She took a silver mirror out of the box. Maggie thought it looked like a mirror that a queen might use.

"This is the mirror my grandmother handed down to me when I was sixteen," said Ms. Chumley.

"My Aunt Martha is so short, she would have to hand things up," said Bonkers.

"How tall was your grandmother, Ms. Chumley?" asked Frank.

"It doesn't matter how tall anybody is, class," said Ms. Chumley. "Handing down just means giving things to someone who is younger than you are."

Maggie noticed that Ms. Chumley's eyebrows were starting to pinch together.

"Let's start over, class," said Ms. Chumley. "An heirloom is something that someone gives to somebody else and then that person gives it to somebody else and so on down the line."

Maggie pictured a whole line of tall and short people passing silver mirrors from one to the other.

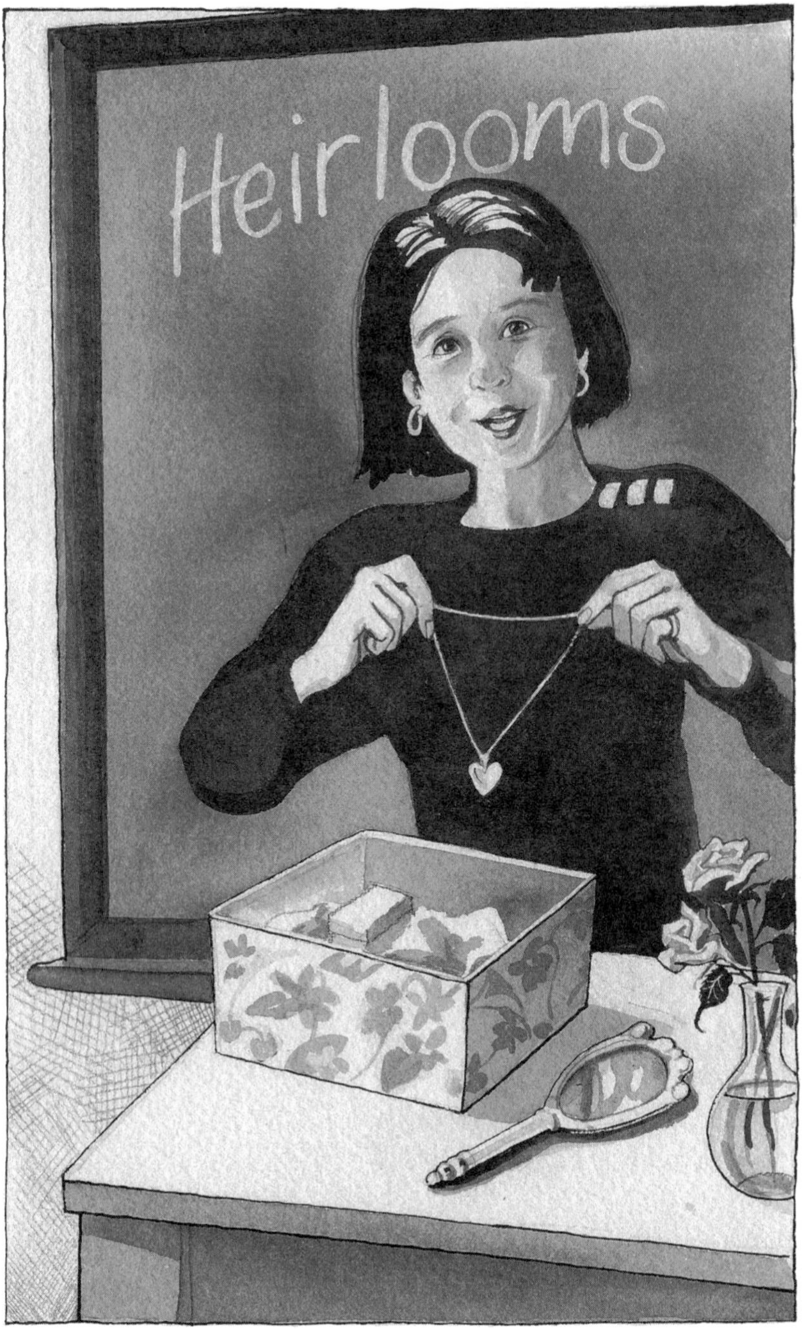
Heirlooms

Ms. Chumley pulled a heart-shaped necklace out of the box. "This is the heirloom locket my Aunt Susan gave me," she said. Inside the locket were pictures of Ms. Chumley as a little girl on one side and her Aunt Susan in a hat on the other.

The whole class ran up to the front of the room to see the locket, and it took a long time for Ms. Chumley to get them back to their desks again.

"An heirloom could be your uncle's watch or maybe even a piece of furniture," said Ms. Chumley.

Maggie pictured someone handing down "pieces" of furniture—a table leg, a dresser drawer handle.

"Could an heirloom be a birthday present?" said Bonkers.

"It could," said Ms. Chumley, "but it doesn't have to be."

"My uncle gave me his lucky tennis shoe," said Frank.

"My aunt gave me her broken bracelet," said Tina.

Ms. Chumley beamed. "That's right, class," she said. "When someone gives you something special that belonged to them, it doesn't matter if they are tall or short, or if they are uncles or grandmothers, or if it's sometimes your birthday and sometimes not"—Ms. Chumley took a deep breath—"we call that an heirloom."

Maggie smiled at Ms. Chumley to let her know the class understood.

"Now, class," said Ms. Chumley, "for your homework tomorrow, I want you to bring an heirloom from *your* family to share with the rest of the class."

"Can I bring my new pink dress?" asked Tina.

"If the dress was handed down to you," said Ms. Chumley.

"You mean a hand-me-down dress is an heirloom?" asked Tina.

Ms. Chumley sighed. "If it's a special hand-me-down."

"Can I bring the puppy my Uncle Matt gave me?" asked Frank.

"No," said Ms. Chumley. "Live things cannot be heirlooms."

"I'm going to bring the diamond ring my grandmother gave me. It's worth a *lot* of money," said Cynthia.

Maggie sighed. Not only did she have to think up a birthday present for Bonkers by Saturday, but now she had to think up an heirloom by Friday. She felt like an old tennis shoe that was definitely not an heirloom.

7

Grams's Attic

Maggie McDougal handed Mikey a red block. "Here, Mikey. These were my favorite blocks, and I am giving them to you. That way if your teacher wants you to bring in an heirloom, it won't be as hard for you as it is for me." Mikey smiled as if he had understood every word.

Maggie put a cooled oatmeal cookie in a plastic bag for Bonkers. Grams's oatmeal cookies were Bonkers's favorite kind, so Maggie always saved him one.

"Hot," said Mikey, holding up his chubby hand like a traffic cop.

"No, not hot," said Maggie. She handed Mikey a cookie and helped Grams plop more cookie dough onto the tray. "I do have the ring that Aunt Patty bought me for Christmas, but it's not old enough to be an heirloom," she said.

"How about an old photograph?"

Maggie looked closely at the picture on the wall of Grams as a little girl. "It's too bad you still don't have this dress," she said. "Ms. Chumley said dresses can be heirlooms."

Grams smiled. "You may be in luck—if I can remember where I put it."

The dress wasn't in the bedroom closet and it wasn't in the basement wardrobe, so they decided to try the attic.

"I forgot what a great place this is!" said Maggie when she pushed open the attic door. The walls were slanted, like the sides of a triangle. Boxes and old furniture were piled all around, and empty picture frames hung on nails.

"Some people call it junk, and some people call it heirlooms," said Grams. "I like to think of it as things to recycle."

Maggie found a wooden train for Mikey to play with.

"Tain," said Mikey. "Grrr."

Grams opened up a huge trunk. Inside there were shawls and shoes and a yellow hat with white flowers.

"Can hats be heirlooms?" asked Maggie.

"I don't see why not, but let's keep looking."

They found a purse made of black beads, and Maggie read a faded newspaper article about when her grandpa had hit a home run with bases loaded.

"Ah," said Grams. "Take a look at this." She handed Maggie something wrapped in tissue paper.

Maggie gulped when she saw the blue dress.

It was made of creamy lace and blue satin, and it had tiny pearl buttons on each sleeve. "Oh, Grams," said Maggie, "it's beautiful."

When Maggie stood in front of the blurry attic mirror, she couldn't stop smiling. "Look, Mikey, it's an heirloom. I look just like Grams in the picture."

"Mmmm," said Mikey seriously, and Maggie knew that meant he liked it.

Maggie put her regular clothes back on and helped Grams organize some of the attic junk. She found a brown hat with a huge feather. "Bonkers would love this hat for playing pirates," she said.

She found an old lantern and a black cape with a silver clasp. "And he would love this cape for playing magician," she said.

Maggie thought about heirlooms. Then she thought about what Grams had said about recycled junk.

"Grams," she said, "I have a great idea—I could recycle some of this stuff to Bonkers

for his birthday. It would cost absolutely nothing."

"Well," said Grams, "since nothing is how much you have to spend, it sounds perfect to me."

Maggie opened another trunk that was filled with books and magazines. Her eyes opened wide. "Did you know there were Green Lizardman comic books in here?"

Grams smiled. "Your father was quite a fan."

"*My* father? The one who never wants to buy me Princess of the Planets stuff?"

"The very same."

"You don't understand, Grams. Bonkers would love these." Maggie sorted through the comic books until she came to one with a huge egg on the cover.

"I can't believe it! This is the original Green Lizardman comic book. Bonkers has wanted this all of his life."

"We'll have to check it out with your father," said Grams, "but I'm sure he won't mind handing that comic book down to you."

"And then I will just hand it right down to Bonkers—a birthday present and an heirloom all at the same time."

Maggie showed Mikey the Green Lizard-man comic book. On page 3, there was a spot where her father had dripped a blob of jelly, and the corner of page 7 had been torn off. She hadn't noticed those things before.

"Oh, Grams, what if Bonkers would rather have a brand-new present that costs a lot of money?"

Maggie thought about the huge present Cynthia said she was going to bring. She thought about how small the comic book would be if she wrapped it. All of a sudden she felt small, too.

8

Ms. Chumley's Brownies

On Friday, Maggie McDougal walked into class wearing her grandmother's blue dress.

"You look like a princess!" screamed Tina.

Everyone crowded around Maggie's desk until Ms. Chumley blew her silver whistle. "You look very special today, Maggie," she said.

Maggie beamed. "It's my heirloom," she said.

"It's lovely," said Ms. Chumley, "but before we share our heirlooms, class, I wanted to tell you about a special treat that we are going to have after recess this afternoon."

On Ms. Chumley's desk was a plate of brownies. "My great-grandmother Lydia lived over a hundred years ago, and these are her brownies," she said.

The class looked at the brownies suspiciously. Maggie could tell Ms. Chumley was surprised.

Finally Frank raised his hand. "I don't think my mother will let me eat anything that's a hundred years old," he said.

Ms. Chumley laughed. "I made these brownies last night," she said, "but I used my great-grandmother Lydia's old recipe. It's been handed down in our family."

Maggie smiled at Ms. Chumley. She was glad they didn't have to eat one-hundred-year-old brownies.

"Cynthia," Ms. Chumley said, "would you show us your heirloom?"

Cynthia walked up and down each row with her hand out so everyone could see her grandmother's diamond ring, but she had already talked about it so much that nobody seemed very interested.

Then Frank showed everybody his uncle's tennis shoe. When he walked by Bonkers's desk, Bonkers held his nose. "Oh, gross," he said cheerfully. "That's the smelliest tennis shoe I ever smelled."

Maggie thought about the pickle juice on Bonkers's card and smiled.

Francine showed her great-grandmother's necklace that had a chain made of real hair.

"It's weird, but interesting," said Tina. It took a long time for Francine to walk around the class.

David showed his Uncle Bob's cracked shaving mug.

"You are so lucky," said Bonkers. All the boys huddled around David's desk until Ms.

Chumley blew her silver whistle. Maggie was glad Bonkers liked the mug even if it was cracked.

Jenny took her heirloom out of a huge plastic garbage bag. "His name is Fooffer," she said.

Cynthia snickered. "Fooffer?"

"I named him when I was a baby," explained Jenny.

"That is the BIGGEST stuffed animal I have ever seen," said Bonkers.

"I have an even bigger stuffed animal at my house," said Cynthia, "and he doesn't have a baby name like Fooffer." Maggie could tell Cynthia was still disappointed that nobody had seemed interested in her ring.

"I don't have an heirloom," said Richard, smiling at Cynthia, "but if I did, it would be a diamond ring." Everybody knew Richard liked Cynthia, but nobody could figure out why.

Maggie could tell that Ms. Chumley was

pleased. "I'm so proud of you," said Ms. Chumley. "These are wonderful heirlooms, and I hope you will hand them down to someone you care about."

Maggie thought about the Green Lizard-man comic book she was going to hand down to Bonkers and about how Bonkers liked the cracked shaving mug. Then she thought about how he liked Fooffer because he was so big and about how big Cynthia's present was. *If only,* she thought. She stopped herself, and then she smiled. If Bonkers wants big, she thought, he's going to get BIG.

9

No More *If Onlys*

"Okay, Grams," said Maggie McDougal, "here's the plan. Bonkers's present needs to be huge. It needs to be BIG—as big as Fooffer."

"I knew you would think of something," said Grams.

Mikey's nose peeked over the edge of the kitchen table. He looked at the cookie dough. "Mmmm," he said significantly.

Maggie grinned. "You're right, Mikey. 'Mmmm' is perfect. Bonkers is not only going to get cookies, but he's going to get them BIG."

Maggie carried a huge cardboard box up from the basement to the living room.

"Come on, Mikey," said Maggie. "You're going to love this." Maggie crumpled up the pages of the Sunday newspaper and told him to put them in the box.

"Dood," Mikey announced. He put more paper in the box.

"*Very* good," said Maggie. She went back into the kitchen and wrapped the Green Lizardman comic book with green wrapping paper.

"Dood," called Mikey from the living room.

"Do you remember when you invented this recipe?" asked Grams, taking cookies off the tray. "You were so little, you kept bunching all the cookie-dough lumps together."

Maggie giggled. "How was I supposed to know the cookies would end up so big?"

"You didn't. But it was a *great* idea."

"Dood dood dood!" shouted Mikey from the living room.

Maggie wrapped the cooled cookies in tinfoil and tied them with a green ribbon. She and Grams took them into the living room.

"Oh, Mikey!" Maggie said.

Mikey stood in the middle of a heap of crumpled newspapers. His face was smeared with black newspaper ink. "Dood," he said proudly.

"As a mess maker," Maggie said, "he is definitely *good*." She spent the rest of the night decorating the big box. She sandwiched Bonkers's presents between crumpled paper, and then she cut out comic strips and pasted them on the outside of the box. She drew funny pictures and put the pickle card in an envelope right on top.

"I think recycling must grow on our family tree," she said.

"It's certainly the most interesting present I've ever seen," said Grams.

"Just as long as nobody thinks it's weird." Maggie sat back and looked at her work. "You know what, Grams?" she said. "I can't wait to go to Bonkers's party."

"Dood," said Mikey. And Maggie thought it was.

10

Happy Burpday!

Maggie McDougal and Grams drove up to Bonkers's house just in time to see Cynthia's mother unloading Cynthia's present. As usual, Cynthia was the first one there.

"Wouldn't you know Cynthia's present would be bigger than mine," Maggie grumbled.

"It's the thought that counts," said Grams, but Maggie was worried.

"If Bonkers hates my present," she said, "I may lose my very best friend."

"I think you can count on Bonkers's

friendship more than that," said Grams.

Maggie sat on the yellow sofa and Cynthia sat on a flowered chair for a long time without saying anything. Cynthia looked at Maggie's present and wrinkled her nose. "That wrapping paper is very weird," she said.

Maggie looked at the fancy gold paper on Cynthia's present. She tried to smile, but her mouth felt as if it weren't working very well. She slid her present so it was half hidden behind the sofa.

Just then Bonkers's father came running into the room with his video camera. "Smile," he shouted. He pointed his video camera at Bonkers who was coming downstairs from his room. He took pictures during the whole party.

"Look at this, Mr. Williams," shouted Frank. When Bonkers's father pointed the video camera in his direction, Frank opened his mouth. Whipped-cream cake came dribbling out.

"That's gross," said Cynthia.

Bonkers smiled at Maggie and Frank. The next time the video camera moved in their direction, they all three opened their mouths and laughed.

After they had eaten, they went into the living room so Bonkers could open his presents. Maggie stood in front of her present, hoping no one would notice it.

Bonkers got a baseball from Frank. "I signed it," said Frank. "It will be worth a lot of money when I'm famous."

"Thanks," said Bonkers. Maggie could tell he liked the baseball.

Bonkers got a book about lizards from David, a Green Lizardman T-shirt from Tina, and a gift certificate from Richard. He saved Cynthia's huge present for last.

"I can hardly wait," said Bonkers as he tore off the gold wrapping paper. But he didn't even have to open the box to see what was inside. The box was bright pink, and in big letters on the side Bonkers read: "PRINCESS OF THE PLANETS SPACE CAPSULE."

Maggie saw Cynthia smile. She remembered how much Bonkers had hated the Princess of the Planets flashlight she had given him. Then Maggie smiled, too.

"I don't believe it," said Bonkers.

"Bradford," said his father, "don't forget to thank Cynthia."

Bonkers rolled his eyes to the ceiling. "Thanks, Cynthia," he said.

"You're welcome," said Cynthia. "I knew you got a Princess of the Planets flashlight last year."

"But maybe you don't know he hated it," said Frank. "A Princess of the Planets Space Capsule? You have got to be kidding." He laughed and pretended to faint on the sofa.

Maggie could tell that Cynthia was upset.

"Hey," said Frank, "there's another present."

Everybody crowded around Maggie's box,

laughing at the comic strips and the funny drawings she had made.

"This is great, Maggie. Thanks."

"It's not the biggest present you got," said Cynthia.

"No," said Bonkers, "but it's the most interesting."

Maggie smiled. She was glad Bonkers liked the way his present was wrapped, but she still didn't know what he would think of what was inside.

Bonkers opened the envelope first. "I smell pickles," he said, and when he read the card out loud, everybody laughed.

"Burp contest!" shouted Frank, and they all burped until they were laughing so hard they couldn't stop.

"Thanks, Maggie," said Bonkers. When Bonkers opened the box, everybody helped him pull out the newspaper.

"Paper fight!" shouted Frank, and he threw the crumpled paper like snowballs.

By the time Bonkers got to the oatmeal cookies, the living room was covered with crumpled newspaper. "These are the biggest oatmeal cookies I have ever seen," he said.

"Grams and I made them," said Maggie.

Bonkers broke apart one of the huge cookies and gave everybody a bite. Maggie was smiling so much her mouth was beginning to hurt. She looked over at Cynthia who wasn't smiling at all.

Bonkers pulled out the rest of the crumpled paper and finally opened the last present inside the box. He didn't say anything for a long time.

"I can't believe it," he said finally.

"It's for real," said Maggie. "The very first Green Lizardman comic book."

Bonkers started running around the crowded living room waving the comic book above his head. Frank slapped him on the back, and everybody crowded around.

Maggie felt like a princess at the happy

ending to a story. She was glad Bonkers liked his present, but she wasn't as happy about Cynthia as she might have been. She walked over to the corner where Cynthia was sitting all by herself. "Don't feel bad, Cynthia," she whispered. "I was the one who gave Bonkers a Princess of the Planets flashlight last year."

Cynthia gave Maggie a quick smile. "Thanks," she said.

"Oh, Maggie," Bonkers said. "This is the best present I ever got in my whole life." He gave Maggie a hug right in front of everybody.

Maggie smiled so hard she nearly had tears in her eyes.

"Happy burpday, Bonkers," she said.

Bonkers smiled back. "This *is* a happy burpday, Maggie," he said. And Maggie McDougal knew that he was right.

Other Springboard Books® You Will Enjoy, Now Available in Paperback:

Angel and Me and the Bayside Bombers by Mary Jane Auch

The Hit-Away Kid by Matt Christopher

The Spy on Third Base by Matt Christopher

A Case for Jenny Archer by Ellen Conford

Jenny Archer, Author by Ellen Conford

A Job for Jenny Archer by Ellen Conford

What's Cooking, Jenny Archer? by Ellen Conford

Wonder Kid Meets the Evil Lunch Snatcher by Lois Duncan

The Monsters of Marble Avenue by Linda Gondosch

Impy for Always by Jackie French Koller

Alex Fitzgerald's Cure for Nightmares by Kathleen Krull

The Bathwater Gang by Jerry Spinelli